Identity Thief

The Causey's Story

Carrie Causey Jackson

Identity Thief
Copyright 2017
By Carrie Causey Jackson

Published by Solutions Press

ISBN: 978-0-9996497-0-1
Printed in USA
Black and White Edition November 2017

Illustrations by Carrie Causey Jackson

Contents

Introduction

The data in this book will be hard to believe. But is true regarding this well-respected young lady. So again, believe this or not.

The story begins with the two of us in the year 2000 month of August. WHO AM I?

Now that is the question.

The girl's, well young lady's, name is Mrs. Sharon Buggica and her husband's name is Mr. Alfonso Buggica.

Getting to the point. This young lady at birth came to be part of a serious experiment as to identity thief (when you illegally take another human identity while within the borders of the United States of America). Let's boil it down and ask this question. Could a baby at birth be placed with another mother who has similar characteristics to the biological mother? Being that these actions take place, the identity thief takes place. The deceased biological mother was not made aware of the exchange. Let's be real here, nor was the alive mother and father made aware that they have been given a deceased mother's offspring, mainly because this situation was perfect for these experiments and their little girl died soon after birth.

The mother is Mrs. Arlean Causey. Her husband Mr. Jefferey Arrie Causey. They are residents of the State of Florida, the capital city of Tallahassee. Both Mr. and Mrs. Causey served two four-year terms in the Army. Mr. Causey became a Pastor and earned his necessary paperwork. His wife went to school after performing her duties at the Army base.

She obtained her Bachelor of Arts Degree, and became a school teacher. They were married four years after serving this country together and re-enlisted four more years while married because of respect for the Army.

The married couple was assigned to McDill Airforce Base in Tampa, Florida, where they served their last four years together, a total of eight years. These respectful people gave their country their lives.

Mrs. Arlean McGrew was 18 years of age when she enlisted in the Army in the hometown where she was born and raised, Tallahassee, Florida. The name given her at birth. Arlean Jean McGrew. Her husband was born in Tampa, Florida. His name at birth is Jerry Arrie Causey.

Jerry was 21 years of age when he enlisted in the Army.

They took slight notice of each other about a year after their enlistment in the Army. Basic Training. They served overseas together, Vietnam here and there for about a year. They came to know of each other on the serious side of knowing each other. By these means they became engaged and married year 2008. Arlean was 22 blessed years of age and now her husband Mr. Jeffrey Arrie Causey, (he prefers to be called Arrie, his middle name, instead of just Jeffrey or Jerry) has obtained 25 blessed years of living.

Once they completed military time served with honors, they relocated back to Arlean's hometown, Tallahassee, Florida. Mr. Jeffrey Arrie Causey was not receiving respect from family or friends because he had chosen to work directly for the Good Lord. They arranged for their first home together as husband and wife in Tallahassee, Florida.

I am Mrs. Arlean Jean Causey, formerly Miss Arlean Jean McGrew. We are truly late bloomers. My husband is Mr. Jeffrey Arrie Causey. I am taking this story from the beginning, to the middle, and the end. Now hold tight readers because this is story is filled with bouncing, rolling, tumbling and any other movements of how I got caught up like this.

By these means of being cautious, you will be able to stay in your saddle and not fall off as you are reading this book.

Here we go. We are on the roll. I am (Mrs. Arlean Causey) 28 years of age and my husband (Mr. Jeffrey Arrie Causey) has been blessed to obtain 31 years of age. The late bloomers, we are stepping into *Identity Thief, The Causey's Story.*

Chapter One

Late Bloomers

It is on for the two of us. Mr. Jeffrey Arrie Causey and Mrs. Arlean Jean Causey. This data refers to our birthdays, which is sort of amazing. We both were born in the same winter season month of January, the first month of the beginning of each blessed year in this United States of America. I was born January 3, 1982 and my husband was born January 4, 1979.

I, Mrs. Arlean Jean Causey, enlisted in the military in year 2000. I stepped into Basic Training here within a small Army Base in Tallahassee, Florida.

This city, Tallahassee, is the capital of Florida.

My enlisting maiden name was Miss Arlean McGrew. My parents are good to go when it comes to our survival. Not a very large biological family on my dad or mom's side. My dad served in the military for four years. He became a Pastor while serving in the Marines. My family lives over our neighborhood church. My parent's address was and still is a ranch in the suburbs of Tallahassee, Florida. They own about 100 acres of land out in these suburbs.

The Church of God is on our land, along with a convenience store and a gas station. Of course, you know there must be a restaurant on this land and there is. Also, dad to this day is a Preacher and a well to do farmer. I am an only child, a female. After I was off into the military, my mom and dad adopted three pretty much thrown away young fellas. Believe this, a set of male twins 14 years of age and their baby brother 12 years of age. These poor little fellas and I truly knew of each other and by the grace of God my parents took them in when their grandmother passed.

Their Dad was killed overseas during the Vietnam War and their granddad drunk himself to death after his only son was blown away.

The mother of the three fellas, who which was an "I cannot take this anymore" mother, drifted off and was announced dead the year 1998 Summer month July. A day after the big Fourth of July. She was found in her room in a rooming house in Tallahassee, Florida. She was said to have poisoned herself or someone else could have given her the last drink.

I was in the eleventh grade, 16 years of age and the twins, Donald and Tyrone were 12 years of age and their baby Brother Johnny was 10 years of age. The grandmother, Mrs. Mary we called her, endured these heartaches and kept her grandsons in order. My dad and mom helped her all the time. The young fellas worked on the farm with dad every cropping season.

My dad's big harvest consisted of watermelons, cantaloupes, corn, sugar cane, tomatoes and white potatoes. My mother had a few rows of green beans, turnip greens, collard greens, green onions, and a few rows of her favorite

home-grown carrots. My dad had all the old, new, and used farming equipment. We also owned horses, chickens, turkeys and ducks. We had citrus trees such as orange trees, grapefruit trees, tangerine trees and a few lemon trees. We also had on our property my mother's mango trees and about two that have lasted, green olive bushes. The elder lady next door to our ranch had given my parents the mangoes and green olive seeds.

Mrs. Mary, the elder lady next door passed, December of year 2000, a few months after I enlisted in the army. I was not able to attend the funeral because she was not family and I was head-over-heels in basic training. My mom, (Mrs. Betty McGrew) the female love of my life, and my dad had decided to adopt the three teenage fellas. These three young men and I had all but grown up to the age I was when I was when

I went into the Military together. These twins came into Mrs. Mary's house when they were two years old. There was NO little brother at that time. I was four years these little creatures' senior. Therefore, I was in second grade. Miss Arlean Jean McGrew. The Kindergarten teacher had me bypass the First Grade, because of my learning so quickly. True that I was an only child and I had Mom and Dad's attention when I asked and sometimes when I did not ask.

I came to know of these little fellas when their dad was killed 1993, September I believe the month was. I know it was a mad ranch of people next to our quite respectful ranch. We had about five trailers of workers living on our property with us. My dad's only brother, they called him Tim, lived in the two-bedroom house next to our barn where our horses and most of our chickens lived. This barn was separate from the storage areas for the equipment for the fields. Uncle Tim was and still is a very handsome man. A Military Marine veteran as well. He married a foreign girl overseas and she was killed. His lifestyles of living now that he is back home. He just moved onto Dad's Ranch, after their parents passed. He has been residing here as long as I can remember. He has had several females come through, but he has not asked any of them for their hand in marriage. There was heavy noise across at Mrs. Mary's Ranch, even sounded like gunshots, some days of the rest of the year 1993. I was carrying the age eleven and the twins, Donald and Tyrone were seven years of age. The baby brother Johnny is very much alive now. Johnny is a fat five years of age and in Kindergarten. The ranch continued to exist. Several times my parents let Mrs. Mary and the three boys sleep in one of our available bedrooms. Finally, granddad next door died from a heart attack year 1997. The blessed windy month of March. I was owning 15 years of blessed teenage years. The twins (Donald and Tyrone) were stepping with eleven blessed years of age and yes, I will include the truly messy baby brother, Johnny. Johnny is hanging on to nine. The want to run away and hide their age. Well, let's go in with the hard hit of this drama, well dramas, at Mrs. Mary's ranch. Okay the "I cannot take this anymore mother" drifted off and was found dead in a rooming house the city of Tallahassee, Florida, the all that and more capital of Florida. The year 1998, July 5.

Okay, their story is told. How these young I believe kind-hearted little three male leeches were adopted by my adorable parents. Alone with the package, the grandmother, Mrs. Mary, had signed over her run-down twenty acres of land ranch to my parents, the McGrews. Dad truly hooked up the two ranches and this is our (Mrs. Arlean Jean Causey and Mr. Jeffrey Arrie Causey) home. Thanks to the Good Lord this ranch is adjoining my blessed parents ranch.

Now my husband, Mr. Jeffrey Arrie Causey, in the past having obtained the age of 21, he had completed two years of some religious college and even when he enlisted in the Army his intentions were to be ordained as a Pastor and he was a few months after we knew we loved each other. Arrie Causey he prefers to be called, especially by me. He did not have a respectful relationship with his older brothers or his younger sister, Miss Carolyn Causey. Arrie did not say hardly anything about his older brothers. Their names are Clarence Causey and George Causey. He said his dad passed from a massive pre-part heart attack. He had served two terms in the Army and died preparing fertilizer at Kaiser Fertilizer Company, located in Tampa, Florida. His family has just broken apart.

His mother remarried. Then she moved to Silas, Alabama. He said he stopped there and checked on her. She was doing well. His sister Carolyn and her husband Jerome relocated to Silas, Alabama with his mother and his older brothers, "God be with them," because they do not know what they are doing to themselves and others that allow them into their lives with the heavy truth of I don't care about myself or anyone else. Arrie finally said these two brothers have helped bring children (sperm donors) because as a daddy they could never own such authority.

Well, the two of us as well as our family and working crew are happy. This is the blessed one year of not in the military lifestyle. I am a good and very happy a few weeks from nine complete months of pregnancy. This is December 25, 2009. Christmas Day. My dad has given his young and outstanding son-in-law his church as the second blessed Pastor. Oh, the Christmas decorations are on. I mean our small ranch is beautiful for the eyes that appreciate the beauty of our blessed Christmas Holiday 2009.

One of my dad's Spanish workers, a lady I have known, sometimes she lives with us now that I am so far alone. I have opened my own little 15-student school for a little special touch for young kids that can't catch what they need to learn quick enough from the teachers of public schools. But I made all the parents aware I am going to close my school's doors until my baby girl make three healthy years of age. My baby shower. I am amazed. All the beautiful (I know you love me like this) gifts from my husband, family, students, friends and even some just business associates. We are all dressed and ready for our Church of God Christmas 2009 morning Blessed services.

The services will be performed by my wonderful God's gift to a woman, my husband. I as well as my live-in housekeeper were ridden to our church on our dad's checkout the ranch motorized carts. We arrived. My husband, my dad (Mr. Bob McGrew) as well as my Uncle Tim and mother (Mrs. Betty McGrew). All people around this part of the Tallahassee, Florida suburbs pretty much attended our Church of God.

There is a very large congregation here this Blessed Christmas Day morning service, year 2009.

We are all seated and I am seated next to my mother in the front row.

The seats are mainly for the Pastors, their wives, and the Deacons and their wives. The other family members of these people can mix and sit wherever in the church. The chorus, all the church members and visitors are standing, singing the opening church song, *The Lord Will Make Away Somehow*. Song completed. We are all seated. My husband is now at the pulpit and he welcomed all the church members and visitors to this Blessed Christmas Day 2009 morning and only church services this blessed day.

Pastor Arrie Causey stated he was new and felt welcomed to his wonderful father-in-law's church, which is now his family church as well, because he and his wife Mrs. Arlean Causey will have the company of a beautiful little girl soon. He went on to say with true courtesy to his new and first church being recognized as Pastor, "I am going to read two Blessed verses of Psalms."

My husband Pastor Arrie Causey is reading:
Psalm 24. The King of Glory entering Zion.

1 The earth is the lord's and all it contains, the world and those who dwell in it.

2 For He has found it upon the Seas, and established it upon the rivers.

3 Who may ascend into the hill of the Lord and who may stand in His holy place?

4 He who has clean hands and a pure Heart, Who has not lifted up his soul to falsehood, and has not sworn deceitfully.

5 He shall receive a blessing from the Lord and the righteousness from the God of his salvation.

6 This is the generation of those who seek Him, who seek thy face-even Jacob Selah.

7 Lift up your heads, O gates,

And be lifted up, O ancient doors,

That the King of Glory may come in!

8 Who is the King of glory?

The Lord strong and mighty, The Lord mighty in battle.

9 Lift up your heads, O gates, and lift them up,

O, ancient doors,

That the King of glory may come in!

10 Who is the King of glory?

The Lord of Hosts,

He is the King of Glory Selah.

Psalm 47

God the King of the Earth.

O, clap your hands, all peoples:

Shout to God with the voice of Joy.

2 For the Lord Most High is to be feared, A great King over all the earth.

3 He subdues peoples under us, and nations under our feet

4 He chose our inheritance for us.

The glory of Jacob whom He loves, Selah.

5 God has ascended with shout, the Lord with the sound of a trumpet.

6 Sing praises to God, sing praises.

7 For God is the King of all the earth Sing praises with skillful psalm.

8 God reigns over the nations, God sits on His Holy Thorn.

9 The Princes of the people have assembled themselves

As the people of the God of Abraham;

For the Shields of the Earth belong to God;

He is highly exalted. AMEN

My wonderful, adorable man has read the respectful words of our Lord within our Bible. I have my eyes locked on my husband (Pastor Arrie Causey) as our Church of God is singing our church closing for the Blessed services. There are no words I can find to express how blessed millions and millions of us humans are to have such a merciful creator that is always there in each human's behalf.

The closing church song, *I am climbing up the rough side of the Mountain*, completed and we are home bound. It is not my imagination. My baby has dropped into the Birth Canal area. Doctor Flynn made me aware, stay close to home and rest as much as I possibly can. Since I made my doctor aware I only want basic pain medication because I had and knew of some bad happenings to newborns because the doctor or doctors subjected the mother or mothers to too much pain medication. I did not know that for whatever reasons me nor my husband will never be told our little girl will die, about 35 minutes after she is born. I will be made aware the baby was healthy. But for some reason, they took a long time before I could see her again. Nor my husband would be made aware of this data until our daughter has graduated from college and married.

Enough of this data before it occurs. I am the mother. I was a little curious about this and that. But these professions had this Identity Thief, covered down to the DNA, if we asked to be tested toward the realness of our baby being ours.

I am home and truly relaxed. Christmas 2009 blew on past, as well as New Year 2010. My birthday, as well as my husband's, passed. My dad, Pastor Leroy McGrew, mother Mrs. Betty McGrew, my blessed husband Pastor Arrie Causey. Mother and Sister are well. It seems to be they are happy this New Year 2010. His brothers are alive still and playing with death.

Time is moving, slow as far as I am concerned. This baby is causing me to be restless. It is time I believe. Today is Thursday, January 23, 2010 and I am truly off to Tallahassee General Hospital.

I am truly in the emergency having a baby area. Delivery room, I believe. Dr Flynn stepped to my bed and made me aware. "Arlean, it will be a few hours before the baby girl arrives." True that. The next day 3:05 am January 24, 2010.

Chapter Two

New Born Baby

January 24, 2010 3:05 am a baby girl came to be alive. This miracle happened at Tallahassee General Hospital. The doctor (the most) Flynn. The patient (glad this hurting drama is done) Mrs. Arlean Causey. Doctor Flynn asked my brave husband if he would like to see his little girl arrive into this world and take her first breath. I am in pain but I heard my husband Mr. Jeffrey Arrie Causey standing over me tell Doctor Flynn, "Sir I would

rather wait outside. My wife is in all this pain and the blood." Strong I am. But when it comes to my baby, giving birth to our baby girl, I will have to leave to keep my sanity in order. I will step out until she is cleaned up. I am in pain but I said alright. Arrie said as he was excusing himself from the room of pain. Arlean your mother and father are here. Well done with the actions from the man that is one of the male loves of my life. Because number one and first my Dad. Second male that made me aware of him as I grew, my Uncle Tim McGrew.

I know the feelings are mutual. My husband is the man our Good Lord created for me to share I believe the rest of my life with.

Dr. Flynn had given me a light sedative for pain and I was a little sleepy after the birth of our little girl and the nurse let me see her as soon as the afterbirth and umbilical cord was cut from the afterbirth. Then Doctor Flynn spanked her and she gave a wake-up call saying, "Don't hit me anymore Doc. I am

alive." Well, all this drama is done. I am cleaned up and patched up. Oh, the Baby Girl's weight is 7 1bs and 5 ounces. My mother named her Sharon Faye Causey. It was almost three hours after my baby girl was born before my husband (Arrie Causey), my mom (Mrs. Betty McGrew), yes, my father too. A Pastor, a loving "and all that and more caring man" (Mr. Leroy McGrew). They brought our little girl into the private room that I am recovering in for me and my husband to share holding her for a few minutes. I let her breast feed for the three days that I am being hospitalized and once home she will be of the modern levels of feeding, the formula.

My husband Arrie is a real military veteran, he said to me as he was about to take a walk around the hospital before going back to our small but straight ranch. My mom and Dad had already gone back home to their I consider huge ranch. My uncle Tim McGrew came by and gave me a big kiss on the cheek and said, "Niece, you truly smell like medicine. I am out of here. I will

see you when you come home Saturday," Uncle Tim said as he walked out of my room door with a little laughter in his voice. I believe that is the 27 of January, also the day of this week is Saturday, later Arlean l love you. Uncle Tim is out of here.

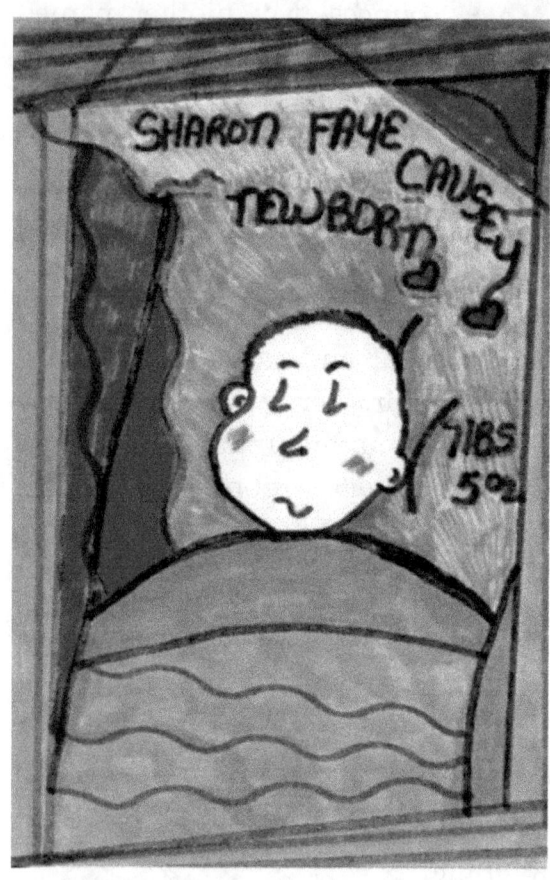

My husband Mr. Jeffrey Arrie Causey said, "Arlean baby, even though our baby girl is newborn and she as well as you are wrapped with this medical hospital smell, you still smell like you are my girl. But our baby girl doesn't have that natural Causey or McGrew odor. Her characteristics are ours. But the smell."

I intervened and said, "Honey she will smell like ours as soon as she is home with us in our familiar smelling nest."

Arrie said, Alright my love." He vacated my room.

Time tends to fly. We are living well thank to our Good Lord, number one. The love and respect my husband and I have for each other, our special little girl. Yes, also the big parts of our livelihoods. My parents the McGrew's have helped us a mighty long way. Arrie's mom and sister came up to see our baby, her granddaughter and his sister (her niece).

They stayed a few days and went back home. This is the year 2012, our Baby Girl, as well as our getting older day has flown by. I am 30 years of age. My real man indeed the Pastor that is Mr. Arrie Causey is 33 blessed years of age.

The last one on this January birth list is our daughter Sharon Faye Causey nickname (my nickname by my husband's words only from him) our Baby Girl. She has grabbed the trying twos. I am the mother of this adorable little girl. You need supernatural powers when your child grabs the trying twos year.

Now a little of my mom and dad's styles of drinking coffee. A little bittersweet black coffee. My mother informed me that the twos and threes are the heaviest growing, learning periods of any child's life. These are their true developing stages, as to them as an individual on this Planet Earth getting ready to own and be responsible for their own actions. But now you and that wonderful husband of yours are responsible for her actions may they be looked upon as good, bad or ugly. My mother finally said, "Baby just take it easy." All these actions are new to her. She knows you and Arrie because of one of the main five senses. The sense of smell. I looked and responded with Sharon now in my arms. I am rocking her in my rocking chair getting her ready for her afternoon nap.

I said, "Mom, maybe this is weird. But she smells somewhat like me and Arrie's normal clean smells after a good bath or shower. But still Mom when this Baby Girl of ours looks at me sometimes I feel distant love as if there is something or someone else she is looking for. There is a look of sadness or loneliness for a minute or so. Then she smiled and giggled a little and the 10k are gone."

My mother said, "Yes indeed is at my house." Well our house and I am a little tired.

This is August; certain fields are in harvest stage. My husband, Dad, Tim and mostly the Spanish Crew are working.

I will start back (My husband and I decided to Tutor, we'll be more like Mentors) working with the kids within my small school on this property when my Baby Girl made five years of age. My mother said, "Arlean you take about an hour or so nap with our Baby Girl."

Today is Friday. The last Friday of the Blessed month of August.

Again, time slipped a little and of course the McGrews, the Causeys and some of our neighborhood ranchers and ranch workers are within the church. God truly blessed America, my dad said Pastor Leroy McGrew, as he stepped from the pulpit and welcomed the second Pastor, the new ordained lead Pastor now.

Open church song *The Lord Will Make Away Somehow* is completed. We are all seated. Thank God, our Baby Girl is napping. But I know she will come back into being awake by the time our one hour or less is done. Sometimes our church service even lasts longer than the regular hour church services in the morning on Sunday. We only have afternoon services on special holidays, such as Thanksgiving, Christmas, New Years and Easter. Pastor Arrie Causey said pay attention to these Blessed words that l am about to use my voice with my English language to share with you, yes Lord.

Then Pastor Causey stated: The main evil four actions that are governed by negative energy forces are: 1. Rulers 2. Principalities 3. Authorities and the last but the heaviest in our society today as well as the past within this blessed United States of America is Number Four: Powers of the dark world. Pay attention Church. God expects His people to believe His promises and to act on them even when circumstances seem overwhelmingly difficult and opposition is fierce. "I believe," Pastor Arrie Causey said, "The Good Lord will straighten out what was left unfinished by appointing elders in every congregation.

"And we like it that yes Lord we can profit from every experience in our life, even the things we do not feel too good about.

"God expects His people to believe His promises and to act on them even when circumstances seem overwhelmingly difficult and opposition is fierce. Fear of circumstances often keeps people from trusting God. It takes a lot of prayerful discernment to be able to see difficult circumstances as opportunities for God to work for his glory instead. Once God makes His will clear to us, He does not expect to hear us say, "I cannot do it."

"He did not accept Moses' excuses or those of the Israelites; neither will He accept ours. Yes Lord, Yes Good Lord, speak through me.

"When we are in Faith, adversity helps us develop strong spiritual muscles. When we fail to walk in faith, God receives no glory. Thank you, Good Lord, thank you, Jesus, One who speaks to the Father in our defense. As you pray, be willing to do whatever God would have you to do for his glory. Yes, Lord speak through me. The three big ones that (giants) most of us face frequently are Guilt, Fear, and Anger. Especially angerR. Church Blessed be thy name in Jesus Christ. AMEN."

Church is closing. There is no closing church song to me (even me and my husband are a little tired). These people are merely exhausted. Homebound. Our baby Sharon (Baby Girl) is now awake and very playful. A quick warm up Sunday dinner. I cleaned our baby up for bed. My husband and I are also in for this Blessed Sunday. The last Sunday of the Month of August. Thank God, the season of fall is almost in. The weather is cooling some.

Well, all is well. We are truly relaxed. I spoke briefly to my parents. My husband Arrie said a few words to my Dad on the phone, of course farming business. Night has stepped to us. Baby sleep, her bed within our bedroom.

We have decided to have her sleep in our room until she is four years of age.

We will tend to our sex needs mostly when she is with my mother, at my mother's house.

Again, time blasted away. This is the year 2015. I am 33 Blessed years of age. Our beautiful daughter, our Baby Girl is a fat Blessed five years of age. Our Baby Girl bedroom is right across the hall from our master bedroom. Our immediate family me, Arrie, Baby Girl and our new animal friend our dog, Stitch. This is a very smart little Vavendor pup. The young man my parents adopted from Mrs. Mary, who used to own this ranch, gave us Stitch.

Me and my husband Arrie are chatting how blessed my past was. The three young men my parents adopted all moved away to Texas, somewhere to some distant uncle that my dad found out about through men gossip. They still recognize my parents as their parents. The phone calls are active since we have been here. Arrie and I, five years that is. They have come through at least once a year with their wives and kids. The twins they are. Donald has two kids. Tyrone has none. Why I don't know. He is married. The youngest brother Johnny is not married. A handsome big time Playboy. He lives in Dallas, Texas and has an agency that handle adults, children actors and actresses.

Well enough about these fellas. But I have to say the eyes don't lie. Johnny came here to celebrate the Fourth of July with us. He brought four people with him. One male bodyguard, two female bodyguards and of course his girlfriend for this 2015 year. I was truly amazed this girl is beautiful. She is African-American, as well as the male bodyguard. Both female

bodyguards are Oriental, Chinese I believe. But I did not ask. This Johnny is in the big money, yes big money. He gave my parents a big 150 thousand dollars and told them to make that church a little larger. Also take a vacation out to Dallas, Texas soon to spend some time on his 100-acre ranch.

"WOW." Believe this, he gave me, his only step-sister, 50 thousand dollars.

And gave our Baby Girl Sharon a gold bar with her full name engraved on top of the bar. Then on the side he engraved these words. His Golden Niece. Wow, this brother of mine was so quiet growing up. He always hung around Uncle Tim. He especially loved and seemed to admire the company of his adopted dad as well as mom. But for real this Johnny was so quiet. He mostly paid attention and just did whatever he was doing without a word. If you asked him something he would answer you and that is that. He hardly ever participated in a conversation. Even at school, he was a straight A student through his entire school term and college. Donald and Tyrone only went to trade school, Tallahassee Vocational Technical School. Johnny graduated with a BA Degree after three years of attending college. He received his Art Degree, the full Art

Degree, paper, pencil, oils, color markers, color pencil, computers etc. Yes, the works of art.

Well, time has a tendency to slip right on away.

This is Thanksgiving Day 2020. I am 38 Blessed years of age and still have an "all that and more" figure. The looks are still hanging on. My husband Pastor Arrie Causey is Blessed 41 years of age. Our Baby Girl a wonderful Blessed truly pretty ten years of age. She is doing well in school. I feel my husband Pastor Arrie and I are blessed to have given life to such a beautiful girl.

But sometimes I can see she truly favors me and her dad. Hard but true, there are times I can see the characteristics of another human. Oh well I thought your imagination does play on you sometime. Well one thing for sure she truly smells of Arrie and me after a quick bath. We are having Thanksgiving dinner at my parents' home. My mother and my live-in maid as well as a few others help us out. They helped us set up the Thanksgiving dinner. The immediate family will have dinner at our dining room table in my parents large dining room. Two other eight-chair tables were set up in the entertainment room.

We did not partake in Thanksgiving morning church service. My husband, dad and Uncle Tim are part of the Thanksgiving 2020 morning service.

Time has enhanced a little. We are off to church. My mother (Mrs. Betty McGrew), some eyes may not agree. But I know we are dressed. I love it when me, my mom and my daughter Sharon have the same color dresses on, as well as the same color shoes. Yes, me and my mom have the same color hats and my daughter ribbons match our hat's colors. We are all in Church. We are seated. A brief opening Church song, *When the Good Lord Calls*. Opening Church song done. Now my brilliant husband Pastor Arrie is standing at the pulpit and he welcomed everyone and wished everyone a Blessed Thanksgiving 2020 and many more blessed years to follow. My husband Pastor Arrie stood silent and looked around the church, at the church people. Then he said, "Church, the Good Lord in Jesus name is allowing me to read and speak from my knowledge these blessed words to you."

On this Blessed Thanksgiving 2020 evening church service. Pastor Arrie Causey is speaking.

"AntiChrist (John 28: 22) The name AntiChrist is the most commonly used title to describe the last great enemy of mankind. The name suggests both his total opposition to Christ and his wicked attempt to counterfeit Christ. The Bible indicates that he will imitate and emulate the true Messiah to deceive men about his true identity. He will try to fulfill the Old Testament prophecies regarding Jewish expectations of the coming Messiah.

"Remember expectations of the coming Messiah. Remember that Jesus himself warned that many will come in my name, saying I am the Christ.

"The False Prophet makes fire come down from heaven in his attempt to fulfill the role of the expected Prophet Elijah as the forerunner of the Messiah.

"The first horseman, the rider on the white horse: The AntiChrist will initially present himself as the great peacemaker. He will deceive many people with a false peace. The First White Horseman on The White Horse is a symbol of the AntiChrist coming in false peace. Notice that he holds a bow with no arrow representing disarmament and peace. Yet he uses peace treaties and agreements to disarm his enemies. The White Horse of False Peace will be followed immediately by the Red Horseman of War, who will take peace from the earth.

"Oh Lord continue to help me deliver these blessed words to my people. Yes, Lord speak through me. Then I stood on the sand of the Sea and I saw a Beast rising up out of the sea, having seven heads and ten horns, on his heads, ten crowns and on his heads a blasphemous name. 'The Beast" is a symbol of the AntiChrist in some passages. In other verses, the symbol of The Beast stands for the ten-nation kingdom with its leader. the number of the beast. here is wisdom. Let him who has understanding calculate the number is 666. AntiChrist will come in my Father's name and you do not receive me. If another comes in his own name, him you will receive. Christ warned Israel that although they rejected him who came in the name of his father, the Jews would one day accept for a time the false claims of the AntiChrist as their promised Messiah. he warned. if another comes in his Own name, him you will receive. Since the prophecies tell us that the AntiChrist will present himself to the Israel as the Messiah, many scholars have concluded that he must be Jewish. Certainly, no religious Jew would dream of accepting a Gentile as the Messiah of Israel. Jesus himself continually warmed of the false Messiah in the last days.

"The Prophet will certainly present himself as the Prophet Elijah and seek to counterfeit his MIRACLE OF BRINGING FIRE DOWN FROM HEAVEN. Obviously, the false prophet must be a Jew to imitate Elijah. The nature of AntiChrist. THE AntiChrist is a liar because his father is Satan, the father of lies. his whole career from beginning to end will be marked by deceit and lies, yet the people will accept his lies because they love darkness rather than light. He is AntiChrist who denies the Father and the Son. The Bible declares that anyone who denies that Jesus is the Messiah is denying the Father and the Son, and has adopted the Spirit of AntiChrist.

"AMEN."

Pastor Arrie Causey stated with love, respect and true kindness with the tone of his voice, passing these words to the church. "Have a Blessed and thankful Thanksgiving 2020. I pray many more to come to every one of you. Again AMEN."

True that. All is well that keeps their house in order. I thought, my truly blessed mother (Mrs. Betty McGrew), my daughter (Sharon Baby Girl Causey), and myself (Mrs. Arlean Jean Causey) are looking very nice in our earth color peace dresses. The three dresses are handmade.

We are all home around the Thanksgiving year 2020 celebration day.

The celebration was brilliant.

Again, time moved quickly and Year 2028 has arrived.

Chapter Three

Baby Girl High School Graduation

Baby girl graduated from Tallahassee High School year 2028.

I am 46 years and my husband Arrie Causey is 49 years of age.

This is the last day of my regular Special School. This Special School allows children to upgrade their learning skills. I gave the younger children their summer year 2028 vacation yesterday June 2nd (Thursday) 2028. The teenagers (you may as well say the young adults) will be excused for the Summer 2028 year today June 3, 2028. Friday this is. Also, my husband (Pastor Arrie Causey) and I (Mrs. Arlean Causey) as well as our daughter (Sharon Faye Causey), yes, her boyfriend Alfonso Buggica (Spanish) as well as seven of our special teenage students. Three females and four males. We are going to take a July Fourth, 2028 vacation in Dallas, Texas on my adopted brother Mr. Johnny McGrew's 100 (luxurious) acres ranch. The works for entertainment. Johnny had made me and my husband aware, with proof, pictures as well as videos. This ranch is truly hooked up. We are flying Delta Airlines. We will be leaving July 1, 2028.

Good news our daughter and her man friend have already registered with Florida A & M. Classes starting the first week of September, year 2028.

Now back to our vacation Dallas, Texas, that is. It is on. This is the last class before our venture to the Longhorn State of Texas. Dallas. Our daughter is over at my mother's ranch. Public School is done. Our Daughter's graduation is on

Saturday June 11, 2028. Our daughter Sharon Faye Causey is an honor student. Her boyfriend Alfonso Buggica is also receiving Honors from the sports area of honor to students that took part in school activities.

Alfonso Buggica was Captain of the Tallahassee High School Football Team. Their School symbol is Tigers.

Our daughter is up and over to her grandparent's ranch on my side of her grandparents. My husband, Pastor Arrie Causey has gone over to the church. The church now because of my brother Johnny's generosity has truly upgraded. The church is now able to house a few more people in need, that Dad will allow additional people to work and live on the property. My dad has housing for five more families. No more than four people per family.

All Children have to be at least nine years of age. Well done with that data.

Class is on. Class consists of seven teenagers, ranging from fifteen years of age to seventeen years of age. Four males and three females. We have a couple of African-American students, who will attend our vacation to Dallas, Texas, a male African American, 16 years of age and the oldest of the students, and an African American female, 17 years of age.

I have all seven of my Special Students' attention, now after a little this and that before I the teacher Mrs. Arlean Jean

Causey start my daily reading to these wonderful young people that want a chance to be successful in this United States of America. I am speaking now. I said students this is a short story about a young lady who found out through experiences utter self-confidence, true respect toward your own existence. But this girl learned do not utter self-confidence if it means that you have to live a lie. Delighted surprised, by a friend that was in need of her kindness. But this male was not her friend indeed. Because of the talk around school, she told him, "You are the one who threatened me with my past. You actually had me believe that I could turn past negative actions to my advantage. (The young lady's stepdad) in order to keep the failure of having it used against me.

"Well this is my past like it or not.

"My upbringing made me what and who I am. Even though I am able to cover some of my cruel experiences traveling this staying alive path. The severity of these tactics that I still recall from time to time. Yes, I know these thoughts will always be with me, a true part of me. It took the mercy of the Good Lord our creator while I was incarcerated to give me the courage to admit that to me, myself and I. All these words stating the lady is somebody because she gave the Good Lord a chance to help heal her hurting soul." Reading completed, now back to my Special Students.

Students when the seven of us plus me, my husband Pastor Arrie Causey, my housemaid, her man (husband?), my daughter and her male friend, that has already asked for her hand in marriage. My husband would not allow engagement, only a promise ring. Pastor Arrie made our daughter aware that he and I were fortunate to have parents such as your mother's parents. He went on to say. Your mother and I grew to learn how to love each other while within the military. Our relationship for each other grew stronger each day, hour, minute or one second we were together or even physically apart and to this day we are holding the same feeling for each other. Finally, my husband told our beautiful daughter Sharon Faye Causey, our Baby Girl in living color, "You and Alfonso attend college together. Once the two of you graduate, well pretty close to graduation, we believe the two of you will pretty much know all there is to know about each other."

Arrie looked at me then at Sharon and said, "Your mother

has already made you aware of the sexual ordeals of protection. Your mother made me aware that you and Alfonso are sexually active. No, No Babies until you first become mentally mature as a well-respected young lady. Because Baby Girl sexual intercourse does not cause maturity."

Well done with what my adorable husband Pastor Arrie Causey had related to our daughter in words. Back to my Special Students.

Students do be respectful ready for our venture to Dallas, Texas July 1st, 2028, Class adjourned. Of course, time passed a little.

Today is Saturday June 11th, 2028. Our daughter Sharon Causey's high school graduation took place. I am carrying (Mrs. Arlean Jean Causey) 46 Blessed years of age. I am now a nice firm size 7 clothing and the grey hair I keep shampooed away.

My husband Pastor Arrie Causey is carrying 49 Blessed years of age. Our loving Baby Girl is 18 Blessed years of age.

True that the graduation from the Tigers Tallahassee High School went very well. Everyone seemed to just let go. We all (even though I rarely indulge with alcohol beverages) my husband and I toasted each other for being a real loving respectful mom and dad to our beautiful daughter. My brother Johnny McGrew had UPS bring our daughter another gift. a full string of small pearls. Wow. Our daughter is amazed, first the engraved gold bar and now a long string of pearls. But we were all blown. The pearls had arrived a day before her graduation. Friday that was, June 10, 2028. As we stepped from the Tallahassee Auditorium, a big red bow was on top of a two-door, mild gold brown color Mercedes Benz in front of the walk out entrance with a big sign that said, "Congratulations Baby Girl You Have Taken the First Big Step into Being a Successful Adult in our Blessed Country the United States of America." This was astounding. There were about ten or more people that Johnny had hired to do this special touch for our daughter. I am crying, my daughter is crying. My husband and dad went over, spoke to the leader of this pack. Seeming everybody is out of the auditorium. Johnny's people had made all these arrangements. Check this out: my parents knew, my husband Pastor Arrie also

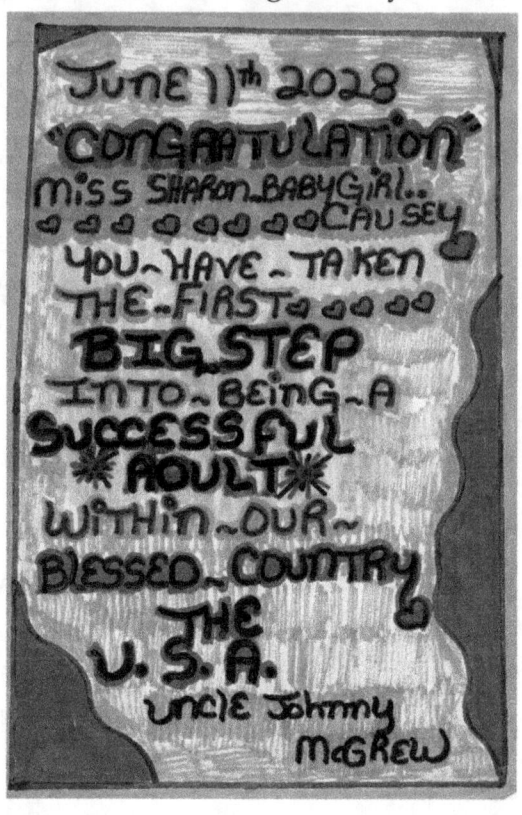

knew. The Limo service transported over 200 hundred high school graduates to the luxurious Hilton Hotel sitting in clear view of the Gulf of Mexico. Our daughter's graduation was that of a very wealthy family daughter graduation. We did and it was done. Time flew.

Today is our adventure day to Dallas, Texas 3 pm flight. We are all at the Tallahassee International Airport, me (Mrs. Causey) the Pastor wife, my husband, Mr. Arrie Causey (The Pastor) Ms. Sharon Baby Girl Causey (The only child a girl of the Pastor Arrie Causey), Mr. Alfonso Buggica (The Pastor Arrie Causey looks like and feels like a son-in-law in a successful few years. Four teenage males and three teenage girls.

Also, the final occupant in our package deal with Delta Airlines is our live-in maid (who came to assist us when she was a teenager from across the water, Mexican, that is). She carried herself as a respectful young lady. My mother had almost raised her. They snuck into this country. About eleven of them had hid on a cargo ship from Mexico to Tallahassee, Florida, she said. All the Mexican people were caught and sent where ever. She had been living with her grandparents. She was taught English by one of her grandmother's white friends that her grandmother still cans fruit for. One of the white men on the ship that knew my parents hid her. My dad went and picked her up from the Tallahassee shipyard. He paid the man well. She came to us and moved in to an adjoining little house by our large home on our property. She married one of the Spanish-speaking fellas that worked and lived on my dad's ranch. They don't have any children. She is about ten years my junior and thirteen years Arrie's junior. She is now 40 years of age. Her name is Mrs. Pamela Martinez. We never knew a last name until she married Alfredo Martinez.

He is five years her senior. Therefore, he is 45 years of age.

We are all aboard the huge 747 Delta Airlines Jet. One flight in about one and one-half hours. We are flying and true that I am like I am still in the military. True that being very cautious and looking out for our crew, as most sergeants are assigned to when traveling. They have orders to look out for their crew until you land or reach land. Okay flying, flying.

We have arrived Dallas, Texas International Airport. We are all here me, my husband, my daughter, Alfonso, and four teenagers, three female teenagers, also my maid and Chauffeur. Mr. and Mrs. Pamela and Alfredo Martinez. We all get into our awaiting transportation to my brother Johnny's 100 huge acres ranch, riding, riding. Believe this five limo styles Mercedes Benz. We are on, now this is true luxury. We have arrived, through the huge gates. My husband and I are in the first Mercedes Benz Limo, as well as my daughter and Alfonso. The other four vehicles, only three were occupied by our crew. The last Benz was occupied with three bodyguards. Believe that huh. Johnny is out on the front of this huge mansion. It is around 8 pm our time back home. True that their time is two hours our junior six pm that is. All 13 of us are residing on the second floor of this huge mansion. This mansion has two full floors, a loft, and a full basement, a huge barnlike building. Another building we were made aware the indoor sports rooms. So, we are truly here and all 13 of us are truly amazed. All is going very, very well. We all I am sure speaking for all of us have never been around living in this much luxury in our entire lives. Yes, growing older True That you say yes, yes, yes, I like it like this.

But me and my husband, we are more settled. We just don't care for too much of the flashy life. Yes, Johnny said, we can retire there and let our kids have our home, well estate (small ranch to grow on). Pastor Arrie Causey said no and of course I agreed with my husband. So, no deal baby brother millionaire Johnny McGrew. We are going back home and time flew. We came in on a Monday July 1, 2028 and the Fourth of July celebration, fireworks, oh my God This brother of mine laid it on us with entertainment. We rode the elaborate horses. We swam even at our ages. My husband and I are still in shape. We have our own fitness room in our home. Recall we are True That Military Veterans. We were going to stay until Monday or Tuesday. My brother's rented Jet is flying us home. So, we will cash our return tickets in. But this did not happen. There came the call from home. My Dad (Pastor Leroy McGrew) died in his sleep last night after he laid down to rest from the Fourth of July bash. We shortened our stay. We all loaded onto the private jet homebound. We arrived. My uncle brought the luxurious bus that is to transport all 13 of us and our luggage home. Sad, I am. But respect to the Good Lord because my dad did not suffer. The Lord let his Soul leave his body the way he had been living. A respectful man indeed.

Today is the 1st Sunday of July 2028 and my dad Pastor McGrew has stepped out of his used-up body. My dad was 72 Blessed years of age when he died. My mother is now 67 Blessed years of age and still able to keep the ranch in order with me and my husband as well as Uncle Tim McGrew's assistance. Check this out, Uncle Tim had married this Mexican girl. Uncle Tim is two years younger than my mother. Therefore, he is 65 years of old age. But

you cannot really put any of us in a ten years of age range of how old we are. Well this Mexican girl is 25 (wow) and check this out. She is pregnant with uncle Tim McGrew's only baby he has ever in his life been accused of. So, they have already moved into the big house with mamma. All them look at me now crying is done. We are within my deceased father's (Pastor Leroy McGrew) church. The church is rightfully my husband's now. Check this out and please get out of here. Alfonso Buggica asked my Dad if he can become a Pastor once he graduates from College. Florida A & M that is. Of course, a big yes dad responded with. We all viewed my dad's well put in order body. Black dresses, huh, not me, nor my mother or daughter. We wore very respectful spring-colored dresses. This is not a sad funeral. Although we all will miss my dad, especially my mom. But he did not actually hold any sickness over three days of his entire time that he was in the company and married to my mother. My mother had told me that my dad woke up during the night about an hour before she realized what he had said to her when he stepped out of the bed, then put on his house shoes and robe. He went outside for about an hour. He had gone over and spoke whatever to his brother Tim McGrew and his new wife. He came back in the house took off his house shoes, still having his robe on, laid back down next to her on top of the covers. Yes, the central air was working very well. He leaned over kissed her and said to my mother, "Honey, tell our son in-law as well as our daughter to keep up their good work. Be sure you make them aware not to be hard on the baby that the Good Lord gave them when they learn the truth. Also, be sure to tell not to even make their daughter aware of the news they had feared for years. I love you Baby."

My mother said he sounded tired and finally said, "Even when my soul steps from this used-up flesh, I am still with you my love, always, always...goodbye baby." He laid back down on his side of the bed. She said about an hour or less he started coughing and coughing. The coughing stopped about 5 am (the clock said, normally when she and her old man are up for coffee before the sunrise). The alarm clock truly woke her up. She is up, Leroy is not, so she went back to the bed, leaned over to kiss him and she did. He was not breathing. He was gone. She called uncle Tim, pastor Arrie causey is reading the final words for my dad that has stepped out of body July 5, 2028. This day at my dad funeral pastor Arrie causey said this wonderful god loving man has turned in his borrowed spirit back to the lord and his soul roams free. We are all aware. We cannot do good things all by ourselves. This man, my blessed father in-law, pastor Leroy McGrew, showed me the real life with humility and gratitude. Yes, these positive energy forces are all around us with us every step of the way. They are in our presents big, huge. When we speak the truth about what god has done to us and for us. Amen.

We buried my dad on his ranch, as his dad, mother and a few other family members had been buried.

Chapter Four

Baby Girl College Graduation

Baby Girl graduated from college year 2032, Florida A&M.

Baby Girl 23 years, Mrs. Causey 50 years and Mr. Causey 53 years.

Time does tend to just move quickly, especially when the Good Lord our creator has blessed you to be a part of such a well knitted family. My dad (pastor Leroy McGrew deceased) says to old and new saying, "All is well that continues well." I (Mrs. Arlean Causey) can witness to that saying when it comes to my blessed deceased father's soul, my dDad (Pastor McGrew) did what he felt he had to do for his family to be straight when the end of his soul within flesh day came.

This is the blessed year 2032. June again. My daughter Miss Sharon (Baby Girl) Causey is graduating from this special college here within Tallahassee, Florida. Florida A&M. I had heard back in the past years most of the students that attended and successfully graduated from this school were African-American. This 21st century year 2032 from what I have acknowledged this college Florida A&M is open with due respect to all Americans of this blessed country. Since all the wars, even certain races of people coming across the water and have tried to terrorize the true "all that and more" citizen of America or

even if you are not a citizen. But still you are residing on the United States of America land spaces. The curiosity that had invaded our country is somewhat caused by American citizens regardless of their race or their status in life, may it be good, bad or ugly. Learning to stick together is the big key and it is truly happening. Our God is a very merciful being.

This Blessed year I (Mrs. Causey) have obtained the half of a hundred years of age 50 that is. My blessed and adorable husband pastor Arrie Causey has obtained age 53 (still looking good to me, and feel good) years of blessed age.

Our daughter (Miss Sharon Causey) is graduating from Florida A&M June 12, (Saturday) 2032 as well as her husband to be soon, Mr. Alfonso Buggica. Our daughter (Baby girl) has obtained the blessed age of 23 years of age. I believe she said her man friend is 24 years of age. Our daughter skipped a grade because such as her mother, she is a very quick learner.

Today is Saturday, June 6, 2032 and I am preparing a small dinner and thinking. Oh, my daughter is wearing the official engagement diamond ring. I still managed to think my life was and still is pretty good. I had always tried to live my life doing good helping others, stopping to visit with others pretending life was alright. Got the point. I Mrs. Arlean Causey, am a God-loving human, but even I get a little pissed off at times, but during these times I present my fake smiles. I think and feel even though I know there is a God and I truly have faith in this superior Being, Guarding Angels as well. Once my soul is out of the flesh, I truly believe I Mrs. Arlean Causey will be able to acknowledge our creator more so than I can within my flesh body. I know if I derive pleasure out of associating with negative energy forces (although sometimes the bad and ugly are necessary to just staying alive), especially when cruel people are trying to play on you because of your decent styles of living. I truly fear the Good Lord knowing that I will have to endure some negative actions to clear myself of these negative energy forces. Regardless, I truly feel that one should now always fear our superior the almighty God.

I was taught to favor the Good Lord's ways. I am finished with the somewhat not so large Saturday snacks, which consists of some devil crabs, cole slaw, fruit salad and some ice tea with fresh lemon juices, of course from our lemon trees.

I am home alone. My husband is over at the church I believe getting ready for church service tomorrow June 7, (Sunday) 2032. My daughter is home. She has moved her belongings home from the Florida A&M College campus. She and a couple of her girlfriends are out getting ready for graduation next Saturday. I am sitting out on our balcony. I am snacking a little and drinking a cold glass of ice tea. I recalled Thursday, just passed day before yesterday, is June 4th, 2032.

Early that Thursday morning, very early before 3 am (my husband was still asleep), the creator spoke to me and said, "I spared your uncle Tim McGrew's life (he was sort of a heavy alcohol drinker) because he has risen above that addiction. But I could not allow him to father a young human, such as the baby his wife was carrying (because of these defaults of character toward substance abuse, uncle Tim McGrew's baby was born dead, years passed) your uncle Tim is still weak and growing stronger. But because of his age, he could fall back to the

addition to alcohol easily." I am truly thinking now, mainly because I know of these actions in reference to my uncle Tim and I truly believe God's Answer is his Word and God's is a promise is always kept.

Well enough of these wonderful memories. My Uncle Tim is a blessed man. Enough of the past. I am still home alone. My husband phoned me from our church and asked me, "Is there a bite to eat around the house, honey?" I responded, "Yes." The Sun is almost about to set. I heard my daughter arrive. She came out to the balcony and made me aware that Florida A&M is having a big dance at the college for the graduating class of 2032. She made me aware she would have a little something to eat, relax a few minutes, shower and dress. Mr. Alfonso Buggica is our daughter's escort, of course.

Now I am back to my idle time reading. I am reading this little religious Biblical pamphlet that I have here with some of my other material that I sometimes relate to when I am relaxing reading:

"We have hope for true life in the eternal Spirit as well as on Earth.

"Nearly 2000 years ago Jesus said. 'I am the way, the truth and the life. No one comes to the Father but through me.' I look at my life and the trials and tribulations that have raged my flesh human body and I realize my heavenly Father has led me on this path for a reason. He is the God who let me fall so low on Earth in

North America to really and truly need him and then comes

close enough for me to feel and see in his chosen adult body human form presence. Since then I truly know I will never be the same on God's green Earth. When the fury of addiction brought many ends to life's roads, almost the human body dead end, grace suddenly surrounded my life. My career has taken a dramatic turn upward. My value now is born again, it is not every day or everyone gets a second chance at life. I heard a statement that we are all signing on the creator credit card. When life's bill comes due only the creator can determine who has paid in full for all humans on the planet Earth. The great thing is the creator charges not any interest. All we have to do is believe and have all of our trust in the creator."

Well done with this special data. My husband Pastor Arrie Causey has arrived home. The sun is down now. It is around 8 pm or so. He ate the small snack for Saturday dinner. There are a variety of goodies. But not large quantities of each.

Our daughter is stepping out to the graduation bash at Florida A&M. I told her to be careful. My husband walked out to her car and made her aware she should wait until Alfonso (her boyfriend) arrives. She should let him drive his van, give her Benz a rest. My husband said he also told her, let your male friend ride you around some. She agreed and called Alfonso. By these respectful means, Alfonso came quickly from their meeting place. My husband told Alfonso Buggica, "You have asked for our daughter's hand in marriage. So, keep that thought in mind when it comes to your fiancée." My husband went on to say, because Alfonso looked at him weird when he said fiancée, so my husband defined fiancée for Alfonso Buggica. He said, "Alfonso, your fiancée our daughter is the young well-reared lady that you are legally engaged to marry." My husband said Alfonso Buggica shook his hand, helped Sharon into his Lincoln Navigator van. Then before he stepped into the driver's seat of his ride, he asked Pastor Arrie Causey,

"Once me and your daughter are married, can I be the second Pastor in your church?" My husband said he was blown away but he gave his soon to be son in-law his approval. They are off and time slid a little.

Today is the Blessed Sunday of the month of June 2032, the 7th day. We are all in our very modern church now. I mean very modern. We even have an area where several people can watch a large screen television, an entire cooking area, an entire nursery for the kids. We are truly blessed. My dad used that large sum of money from his adopted son Johnny McGrew to enlarge this church. By these blessed means, my dad opened doors for more jobs and more housing for needy people.

My adorable husband Pastor Arrie Causey is standing at his pulpit now. He has not acknowledged a second pastor. The two of us know that our son in-law will fill the second pastor spot. Opening church song is done. My mother, daughter and I are seated in the pastor's family area on the front row. Alfonso Buggica, Tim and his wife are on the second row. Our house keepers Mr. and Mrs. Martinez are seated on the last row of the entrance into our church. My husband Pastor Arrie Causey said he feel that reading some verses from our Bible will calm a lot of us down during this very, very hot summer time of this year 2032.

Pastor Arrie Causey is reading.

Psalm 117

A psalm of praise

1 Praise the Lord, all nations; laud him, all people;

2 For his loving kindness is great toward us, and the truth of the Lord everlasting, praise the Lord!

Psalm 118

Thanksgiving of the Lord's saving goodness.

1 Give thanks to the Lord, for he is good; for his loving kindness is everlasting

2 Oh let Israel say, his loving kindness is ever lasting

3 Oh let the house of Aaron his lovingkindness is everlasting

4. Oh let those who fear the Lord say, his loving kindness is everlasting

5. From my distress I called upon the Lord; the Lord answered

Me and set me in a large place,

6. The Lord is for me; I will not fear; what can man do to me?

7. The Lord is for me among those who help me. Therefore, I shall look with satisfaction on those who hate me.

8. It is better to take refuge in the Lord, than to trust man.

9. It is better to take refuge in the Lord than to trust in the princes.

10 All nations surrounded me; in the name of the Lord I will surely cut them off.

11 They surrounded me, yes, they surrounded me; in the name of the Lord I will surely cut them off.

12 They surrounded me like bees; they were extinguished as a fire of thorns; in the name of the Lord, I will surely cut them off.

13 You pushed me violently so that I was falling, but the Lord helped me.

14 The Lord is my strength and song, and he has become my salvation.

15 The sound of joyful shouting and salvation is in the tents of the righteous; the right hand of the Lord does valiantly.

16 The right hand of the Lord is exalted; the right hand of the lord does valiantly.

AMEN

My husband has stepped down from the pulpit back into his office area. We sing the closing song for our church, titled "We love the Lord" church closing song done. I knew my husband Pastor Arrie Causey would be home later. Our son-in-law to be soon was approached by my uncle Tim McGrew and told my husband Pastor Arrie Causey would like to speak with him in his office.

Well again time simply made it to our blessed daughter's (Sharon Baby Girl Causey) graduation day. We are all at the Tallahassee Auditorium this Saturday, June 12, 2032. The are waiting to be seated and called one at a time to receive their (I believe hard-earned) Degrees. All went well in reference to this event. The entire family was surprised to see our brother, uncle and son show up unannounced. The graduation bash was truly on at the end of the line of students, well when and after the last student received his or her degree. Our son-in-law to be soon had asked the authority people of Florida A&M if he could recite Psalm 23 and by reciting these blessed verses this would be the closing of June 12, 2032 graduation. Yes, they gave him permission. Now our son-in-law to be has been granted the attention of the entire 1,000 or more people attending and now Mr. Alfonso Buggica is speaking the Psalm 23rd:

Psalm 23

The Lord the psalmists shepherd.

1 The Lord is my shepherd, I shall not want.

2 He makes me lie down in green pastures; he leads me beside quiet waters.

3 He restores my soul; he guides me in the paths of righteousness for his name's sake;

4 Even though I walk through the valley of the shadow of death, I fear no evil; thou art with me; thy rod and thy staff, they comfort me.

5 Thou dost prepare a table before me in the presence of my enemies; my cup overflows.

6 Surely goodness and loving kindness will follow me all the days of my life, and I will dwell in the house of the Lord forever.

Thank you, church, thank you.

The June 12, 2032 graduation is done. We have prepared a small relaxing party for my daughter and her closest friends. Well let me put it like this. My husband Pastor Arrie Causey and my mother Mrs. Betty McGrew plus Big Money, Mr. Johnny (Play Boy) McGrew has done the do. The party was on. My

husband even had a toast of a glass of expensive wine that my big pocket brother Johnny had toasted to Mr. Alfonso Buggica, Sharon (Baby Girl) Causey and of course the entire family, and employees. A big congratulation to the class from Florida A&M June 1 2th, 2032 Class Graduation.

Well I (Mrs. Arlean Causey) must say, "All is well that began well and continues to function well."

Chapter Five

Daughter Wedding

Wedding Bells June 18, 2033

The Lord will make a way somehow. (All that believing and respect this Superior Being is aware). He might not be there

when you want Him but the Creator and Guardian Positive Angels are always right on time.

All the do's have been done. We are all seated in our Church. My husband Pastor Arrie Causey has the honor to wed our daughter and Mr. Alfonso Buggica this June 1, 2033, a beautiful summer Saturday in the Sunshine State of Florida's, Capital City Tallahassee. All is very quiet within the church now.

Our children are saying their marriage vows to each other, now Pastor Arrie asked the Church, "If there is anyone against or do not approve of this marriage let him or her speak now or forever hold your peace."

I, Mrs. Arlean Causey is in thought land, I am thinking normally a mother can see herself at younger and vulnerable ages in their daughter or daughters. But why I don't know.

I could never see myself in my daughter's (Sharon Causey) frame, Why? Now believe this if you care to. A silly action, my brother Johnny (Big Pocket) McGrew stood up and said (yes he is a little silly) "Reverend I approve this Marriage. So, hurry this marriage up so we can have a little fun here before me and mine step back to Dallas, Texas. Thank You, Thank You." Uncle Johnny's last words before he took his seat again. These (I don't know what to say or refer to them as), started clapping their hands making my husband Pastor Arrie Causey know they approved, so hurry up.

Pastor Arrie Causey acknowledged the hurry up ordeal. Pastor Arrie Causey started with a little smile on his face, as well as Sharon and Alfonso were smiling. "Mr. Alfonso Buggica, you may kiss your Bride, Mrs. Sharon Buggica."

Oh, the ring had been put on her finger before the kissing (smile) marriage done. My husband Pastor Arrie Causey had said also before they kissed the big, big words: I now

pronounce you husband and wife in the name of the lord, until death do you part. Amen.

Done, done, done.

Sharon threw her bouquet. One of our ranch hands' daughter caught the flowers. Alfonso and Sharon are spending their two weeks honeymoon on Uncle Johnny (Big Pocket) McGrew's ranch. Both of our children, Alfonso and Sharon, have obtained enough credits from College to perform as I performed school teachers.

My husband Pastor Arrie, uncle Tim and most of the other ranchers pitched in financially to pay for converting 50 acres of our ranch farmland into a School. They have almost completed a school ranging from first grade to twelfth grade. Also, five special classes for kids such as I teach with learning disabilities. The school is large enough to cover at least 100 students. So as of August, the last week our public-school addition to this country will be open. The school name is (in due respect to our daddy and my loving respectful husband Pastor Arrie Causey) McGrew's Causey's Way's School.

Well, all is well that begins and functions well so that you will be able to end well once your soul steps out of the flesh body it now resides within.

My daughter Mrs. Sharon Buggica, her husband Mr. Alfonso Buggica, two of our security people, my brother Johnny (Play Boy) McGrew, his girlfriend Miss Vivian and two of his security people, departed early Sunday morning.

This is Sunday, June 19, 2033. Our daughter married at the age 24 and her husband 25 blessed years of age. I am 51 years of age and my husband Pastor Arrie is 54 blessed years of age. Time moved a little this Blessed Sunday.

Because of the airport ordeals, yes going to the airport to see our family off on their honeymoon at my brother Johnny (Play Boy) McGrew's ranch. We did not attend morning church

service. Therefore, we are now within evening church service. We are all seated and church service begins. Pastor Arrie Causey bypassed the opening church song and made the

announcement to the church that our son-in-law Pastor Alfonso Buggica will serve as our Church Second Pastor. My husband smiled and said, "He speaks fluent English, also fluent Spanish." Then my husband said also, "Our son-in-law has been assigned by the authority of these ranchers of our community to take the job of the principal of our school, also our daughter Mrs. Sharon Buggica will perform as the assistant principal. Experience is not the issue here; respectful love and kindness is. We exist among several races. All of us because of respect, kindness, love have mixed and are living well together.

"So be it." That is why these two young people will govern our school, McGrew's Causey's Way's School. Now my husband Pastor Arrie Causey stated that he will read several Blessed Verses from our Bible. After these readings, church will be adjourned on this Blessed Sunday June 19, 2033.

Pastor Arrie Causey is reading verses from our Bible:

Psalm 120
Prayer for deliverance from the treacherous

In my trouble, I cried to the Lord. And he answered me.

Deliver my soul, O Lord, from lying lips, from a deceitful tongue.

What shall be given to you, and what more shall be done to you, you deceitful tongue?

Sharp arrows of the warrior, with the burning coals of the broom tree.

Woe is me, for I sojourn in Meshech, for I dwell among the tents of Kedari

Too long has my soul had its dwelling with those who hate peace.

I am for peace, but when I speak, they are for war.

Yes, Good Lord, let me continue to read these Blessed Verses to all of the people of this Church this Blessed Sunday June 19, 2033. Oh Lord please continue to speak through me.

Psalm 121

The Lord the keeper of Israel

Will lift up my eyes to the mountains; from whence shall my help come?

My help comes from the Lord, who made Heaven and Earth.

He will not allow your foot to slip; he who keeps you will not slumber.

Behold, he who keeps Israel, will neither slumber nor sleep.

The Lord is your keeper; the Lord is your shade on your right hand.

The sun will not smite you by day, nor the moon by night.

The Lord will protect you from all evil, he will keep your soul.

The Lord will guard your going out and your coming in.

From this time forth and forever;

Yes, Lord yes Lord

Psalm 122

Prayer for the peace of Jerusalem

Was glad when they said to me, "Let us go to the house of the Lord."

Our feet are standing within your gates

Jerusalem, that is built as a city that is compact together;

To which the tribes go up, even the tribes of the Lord. An ordinance for Israel to give thanks to the name of the Lord.

For there thrones were set for judgment, the thrones of the house of David.

Pray for the peace of Jerusalem. "May they prosper who love you."

"May peace be within your walls, and prosperity within

Your palaces."

For the sake of my brothers and my friends, I will now say, "May peace be within you."

For the sake of the house of the Lord our God 1 will seek your good.

Oh Lord, continue to speak through me by continuing to let me speak these Blessed words from these verses to my Church.

Psalm 123

Prayer for the lord's help

To thee I lift up my eyes, O thou who art enthroned in the heavens!

Behold, as the eyes of servants look in the hand of their master to the hand of her mistress; so our eyes look to the Lord our God, until He shall be gracious to us.

Be gracious to us, O Lord, be gracious to us; for we are greatly filled with contempt.

Our soul is greatly filled with the scoffing of those who are at ease, and with the contempt of the proud.

Yes, Lord speak through me.

Psalm 124

Praise for rescue rom enemies.

"Had it not been the Lord who was on our side," let Israel now say.

"Had it not been the Lord who was on our side when men rose up against us;

"Then they would have swallowed us alive, when their anger was kindled against us;

"Then the waters would have engulfed us. The stream would have swept over our soul;

"Then the raging waters would have swept over our soul."

Blessed be the Lord, who has not given us to be torn by their teeth.

Our soul has escaped as a bird out of the snare of the trapper; the snare is broken and we have escaped.

Our help is in the name of the Lord, who made heaven and earth.

Psalm 125

The Lord surrounds this people.

Those who trust in the Lord are as Mount Zion, which cannot be moved, but abides forever.

As the mountains surround Jerusalem, so the Lord

Surrounds his people, from this time forth and forever.

For the scepter of wickedness shall not rest upon the land of the righteous; that the righteous may not put forth their hands to do wrong.

Do good, O Lord, to those who are good, and to those who are upright in their hearts.

But as for those who turn aside to their crooked ways the Lord will lead them away with the doers of iniquity. Peace be upon Israel.

Yes, Lord keep my eyes on these Blessed pages, so I can continue to have you speak through me, by reading these verses to my Church.

Psalm 126

Thanksgiving from return from captivity.

When the Lord brought back the captive ones of Zion, we were like those who dream.

Then our mouth was filled with laughter, and our

Tongue with joyful shouting; then they said among the nations,
"The Lord has done great things for them."
The lord has done great things for us; we are glad.
Restore our captivity, O Lord, as the streams in the south.
Those who sow in tears shall reap with joyful shouting.
He who goes to and fro weeping, carrying his bag of seed, shall
indeed come again with a shout of joy, bringing his sheaves with him.
Amen

Yes, Good Lord, this has been a very tiring day for my family getting our daughter off to her honeymoon, upon my brother-in-law Mr. Johnny (Big Pocket) McGrew's ranch.

We are all home bound. It seems like everybody in this church service also looks somewhat worn out. By these means, I am truly happy that time slipped right on away.

Today is Monday August the 24, 2033. My daughter and Alfonso Buggica came back home last Saturday. Mr. & Mrs. Buggica are now living in the big house.

Today is the first day of our blessed school, McGrew's, Causey's, Way's. Our son-in-law Pastor Alfonso Buggica is principal and our daughter (Mrs. Sharon Buggica) is the assistant principal. I stayed clear of these jobs, because I have obtained my 51 years of age and my blessed husband Pastor Arrie Causey has obtained 54 blessed years of age. My husband and I hired the staff for this school. Twelves grades are acknowledged here. Therefore, there are two teachers per grade level. Therefore, we hired twenty-four teachers. A few whites, a few African-Americans and a few Spanish. We have it going on. We have the stuff at the school. This campus is loaded. A gym, basketball and many other games can be played within this large gym. Also, an indoor pool area, a track, tennis court, even a nine-hole golf course, since back in the past of Mr. Successful Tiger Woods, a lot of young people need more than just football, basketball and baseball. The gym, getting to the point, consists of just regular basic games, such as cards, dominoes, ping pong, and drawing classes, the works with art even, writing classes.

It is on within this elaborate blessed school McGrew's Causey's Way's.

We have 200 seating spaces in this school auditorium. Yes, Yes, the Good Lord has been so merciful to every last one of us within this school McGrew's Causey's Way's Auditorium. Today, August 24, 2033, we are all here, especially the adults that cared to be seated and Pastor and Principal Alfonso Buggica, Mrs. Sharon Buggica, also the Dean of Boys and the Dean of Girls and the four school counselors. We also have assigned to this school two doctors (mental and physical), also four nurses (two mental and two physical). Also, a dentist and an eye doctor. We have our clinic stuff set up for these wonderful children. The clinic also assists our ranch working adults and even some young people that don't attend this special school or adults that are not employed on our ranch. We had converted about ten more acres of our land for the medical addition. Yes, the clinic.

Although the workers did respect our wishes as to the trees and a spring of fresh water here and there. because we did not want to just pour concrete and clear nature off this ranch.

We are all seated. We sing our school song, one of our special church songs, *God will Make a Way Somehow*. Again, we are all seated and our blessed son-in-law Pastor Principal Alfonso Buggica stands up. He made us aware he is going to read the Psalm 23 from his Bible for the official opening of this school. (There are a few noise jobs around. newspapers, a couple of TV stations,)

Pastor Alfonso Buggica is reading:

Psalm 23

The lord, the psalmist's shepherd.

The Lord is my shepherd, I shall not want.

He makes me lie down in green pastures; he leads me beside quiet waters.

He restores my soul; he guides me in the paths of righteousness for his name's sake.

Even though I walk through the valley of the shadow of death, I fear no evil; for thou art with me; thy rod and thy staff, they comfort me:

Thou dost prepare a table before me in the presence of my

Enemies; thou hast anointed my head with oil; my cup overflows.

Surely goodness and loving kindness will follow me all the days of my life, and I will dwell in the house of the Lord forever.

Amen

The Pastor said over the loudspeakers, even louder than when he read the Psalm 23, "May the Good Lord be with all of you and let's grab what you need in order to step back into regular school. If you choose. Because you can obtain a respectful high school diploma right here at McGrew's Causey's Way's School. Let our staff know if you need a little more than what your teachers are teaching."

Assembly done and again time flew by.

Today is August 30, 2033. Almost the last day of this month. 30 August 2033 is Sunday.

True That. We are all in our beautiful church. Thanks to my whatever labels towards being Rich Baby Brother Mr. Johnny McGrew.

Today August 30, 2033 instead of my husband covering the pulpit, the second assigned Pastor will take that job this blessed day. Pastor Alfonso Buggica welcomed all the students that came to church service today and the adults, as well. He went on to say that his wife (our daughter) is with a child. Scheduled to take existence on this Planet Earth a true Spring young man. The blessed month of May.

Sharon had made me and her dad aware that she picked up more than luxury fun on her honeymoon. She also had her eggs fertilized by her husband Pastor Alfonso Buggica.

Me as well as my husband, also my mom are very happy. The first child is a male child, that new levels have been broken by our daughter (or is she really our daughter). The last 100 years or so of my mom's blood line, the first baby has always been a female.

The opening church song is done and now Pastor Buggica is reading from Psalms verses as his father-in-law respects of reading the Bible to our church.

He is reading:

Psalm 127
Prosperity comes from the Lord.
Unless the Lord builds the house, they labor in vain who build it; unless the Lord guards the city, the watchman keeps awake in vain.
It is vain for you to rise up early, to retire late, to eat the bread of painful labors; for he gives to his beloved even in his sleep.
Behold children are a gift of God (the good Lord the fruit of the womb is a reward.
Like arrows in the hand of a warrior,
How blessed is the man whose quiver is full of them; they shall not be ashamed, when they speak with their enemies in the gate.

Oh, Good Lord continue to speak through me.

Psalm 128

Blessedness of the fear of the Lord:

How blessed is everyone who fears the Lord who walks in his ways.

When you shall eat of the fruit of your hands, you will be happy and it will be well with you.

Your wife shall be like a fruitful vine, within your house, your children like olive plants around your table.

Behold, for thus shall the man be blessed who fears the Lord.

The Lord bless you from Zion, and may you see the prosperity of Jerusalem all the days of your life.

Indeed, may you see your children's children.

Peace be upon Israel

Keep me reading these Blessed Verses Good Lord.

Psalm 129

Prayer for the overthrow of Zion's enemies.

"Many times, they have persecuted me from my youth up; yet they have not prevailed against me.

Let Israel of the message how could I?

The plower plowed upon my back; they lengthened their furrows."

The Lord is righteous; he has cut in two the cords of the wicked.

May all who hate Zion be put to shame and turned backward,

Let them be like grass upon the housetops, which withers before it grows up;

With which the reaper does not fill his hands, or the binder of sheaves his bosom;

Nor do those who pass by say, "the blessing or the lord be upon you;"

Yes, Good Lord, yes Good Lord.

Psalm 130

Hope in the Lords forgiving love.

Out of the depths I have cried to thee o Lord

Lord hear my voice I let thine ears be attentive to the voice of my supplications.

If thou Lord, shouldst mark iniquities, O Lord, who could stand?
But there is forgiveness with thee, that thou mayest be feared
I wait for the Lord, my soul does wait, and in his word do I hope.
My soul waits for the Lord more than the watchmen for the Morning.
0 Israel, hope in the lord; for with the Lord there is lovingkindness, and with him is abundant redemption.
And he will redeem Israel from all his iniquities.
Amen

O Lord thanks for speaking through me this Blessed Day.

Closing church song. *I am Climbing up the Rough Side of the Mountain.* Closing church song done. We (my husband and I as well as my mom and uncle Tim and his wife) congratulated him for his first church service as a Pastor and also a wonderful principal and our daughter (Mrs. Sharon Buggica) his wife for the school works they are governing. A wonderful dinner at my mother and their home bringing in this wonderful Fall season of 2033.

Time simply blew away.

Today is Christmas 2033. True that both houses have all that and more when it comes to Christmas decorations. Our daughter (Mrs. Buggica) is five months pregnant.

All goes well, when you love the lord, in order to respect and love yourself.

Chapter Six

Made Aware of Identity Thief

Year 2034
This is real stuff "all that and more."

I, Mrs. Arlean Jean Causey, a blessed 52 years of age, Pastor Jeffrey Arrie Causey, a blessed 55 years of age, our Baby Girl Mrs. Sharon Faye Causey Buggica (a little grandbaby due April of this blessed year) and our son-in-law Pastor, Principal Alfonso Buggica. Now this is the real deal. Being the mother, I thought, I wondered, I dreamt, I saw signs, I felt signs, and there were several times as a baby when there was eye to eye contact between the two of us. I knew she was looking for someone else. But this truth will not set me or my husband Pastor Arrie Causey, free because we love and adore our beautiful Baby Girl from day one and me as well as my respectful loving husband.

I believe I will love this girl (Mrs. Sharon Baby Girl Causey Buggica) as long as there is existence within this universe that we are a part of. My husband Pastor Arrie Causey and I are aware that life still exists even after our soul and borrowed spirits leave the flesh (body), dead, deceased, done with flesh life and mercifully the soul, your soul is out of body but still very much alive.

Here is the amazing truth even after we endured rearing someone else's biological offspring, although not our human flesh and blood. I as well as my husband Pastor Arrie know our creator intended my husband and I to parent this beautiful girl.

We received a call one day after Christmas 2033, of course December 20, 2033 by using our open phone calls box. We were both able to acknowledge the reasons these two strangers have phoned our home.

They had informed us that they have some very important data about our daughter, our only child. Of course, we are upset. But the female spoke and said, "The news is very pleasant Mrs. Causey." New Year's Day it will be. Our son-in-law and daughter are not moving about very much. Our daughter a real five months Pregnant. She has quite a bit of weight other than just the stomach. My body was neat and firm all the way throughout my pregnancy. But different strokes for different folks. Smile. Our daughter closed down her job to an out of the house assistant principal, when she stepped to five months. She had been in the hospital twice already because she had noticed a few drops of blood when she made her fifth month of pregnancy. My daughter's doctor, a female specialist, informed her to get total relaxation, physically and mentally. She would have to take these actions the remainder of her pregnancy. She walked around a little. But she cannot even do a lot of walking. She cannot drive. She is truly uptight. But she told me and asked me, was my pregnancy this delicate? Like a true "Shut Down" for the pregnant mother. I made her

aware I was very active. A lot more active than maybe I should have been. Well it is on us. We brought New Year 2034 in together with our family, close friends and some of our close associates. New Year's Day is on. I believe everyone is in their own home now truly relaxing at their best. Our live-in maid and chauffeur are out taking some time with some of their friends that do not work for us or with us.

They have arrived. They pulled up in a Mercedes Benz Limo (slang: Get Out Of Here) My husband had some of the fellas keep eyes out for us. Because these people are extremely financially secure. One of our respectful male workers escorted these two white people (male and female). The chauffeur remained in the Limo.

They are within our home now, very pleasant people. There is no harsh feeling about these two people. These two people address themselves as "unknowns," Male and Female. The Unknowns made us aware that we are not the biological parents of our beautiful well-reared daughter. The Unknowns made us aware of the experiments. The Unknowns were very satisfied with our levels of parenting, they went on to say. My husband Pastor Arrie Causey and I, Mrs.

Arlean Causey, are not the only people that participated with these experiments. There are thousands of American citizens in different states of this United States of America. They made us aware only one hundred and eleven people, cleared the experiments with more than the word respect could account for. The female Unknown is silent now. The male Unknown said we are sure our creator meant some of these children to be raised by adequate role models such as yourselves. Finally, the male Unknown said, "We, the well establishment titled Unknowns, have a reasonable donation for the two of you, Mr. & Mrs. Causey. The United States of America currency dollars amount if 50 million dollars. The two of you are welcome, (so says our establishment) to function as the two of you see fit with the donation. But we ask of you (Mr. & Mrs. Causey) as well as all the other people that were subjected to our experiments, this is our secret."

They went on to say before they departed our Ranch. they will continue these actions. But now they have enough data (as to certain levels of humans) to know what levels of humans such as role models to submit these "all alone offspring" with the quickness a small certified check. The check had the appearance of a SSI or SSD Check. It appeared to be a Federal Government check. They were out of our house, off our ranch and wherever. But they will never ever be out of our lives. Because these Unknowns presented us with actions that few humans ever dream about.

Well time is truly passing. The month of January 2034 is of the last blessed week. Our daughter, Mrs. Sharon Buggica, is now a truly blessed 26 years of age on a day such as this and January 24, 2034 because we had been chosen for this experiment by the Unknowns. We invited all the family and some of the leaders of our ranch staff to a gathering at our church, within our ranch meeting quarters. We are all seated around this long table. My husband Pastor Jeffrey Arrie Causey has the floor. He stood and said, "Can I have all of the people asked to be here seated at this table attention. Today is our Baby Girl's (Mrs. Sharon Buggica) birthday."

My husband went on say, "Because my wife and I have been blessed with a huge donation from a very caring establishment of our government, my wife and I have decided to spend the rest of our blessed days relaxing and thanking our Good Lord for making our ways possible.

Uncle Tim McGrew has accepted the rights to govern the ranch. By these means, so he can afford more staff and upgrade some of the staff already here with a little more convenience, we are donating to him for our family ranch to remain in order ten million dollars (everyone is very, very quiet now and my Uncle Tim has the "Big Eyes"), one million to our live in maid and chauffeur, even if they are not to stay on our ranch, twenty million to our daughter, her husband and soon a male addition to their family, as well as our as thanks to the Good Lord Grandparents. We have spoken with Mr. Johnny (Big Pocket) McGrew because the remaining millions will secure my wife, mother-in-law and I a very relaxing retirement.

Meeting adjourned. Everyone seems very happy. My husband sent his mother and sister a money draft for eight million dollars. Then my husband kept saying (thinking out loud), "Why should I?" He finally gave in to his feeling and respect for his biological brother that is still alive and not drinking anymore. He sent his brother a money draft for one million dollars. His older brother Clarence had passed a few years back.

Time flew. Today is April I, 2034. Everybody plays the fool sometime. There are no exceptions to the rules. A seven-pound five-ounce Baby Boy. This Baby Boy has been born. My Baby Brother Johnny set housing up for us. We have the second small mansion on his estate. Yes me, Arrie, Sharon, Alfonso Sr., and

Alfonso Jr., my mother and two of our real helpers all relocated to our new home, Dallas, Texas, July 1, 2034.